Simone's Letters

Dear Mr Cakebread . . . For starters my name is Simone, not Simon . . . Mum says you sound just like my dad. My dad, Dennis, lives in Bartock with his girlfriend, Alexis . . . My mum says lots of rude things about her because Alexis was one of the reasons my parents got divorced (I was the other) . . .

When ten-year-old Simone starts writing letters to Jem Cakebread, the leading man of a touring theatre company, she begins a friendship that will change her life . . . and the lives of all around her: her mum, her best friend Chloe, her new friend Melanie—and not forgetting Jem himself!

This collection of funny and often touching letters charts Simone's final year at Primary School; from a school visit to *Rumpelstiltskin's Revenge* to her final leaving Assembly; through the ups and downs of her friendships—and those of her mum and dad.

HELENA PIELICHATY was born in Sweden to an English mother and Polish-Russian father. Her family moved to Yorkshire when Helena was five where she lived until qualifying as a teacher from Bretton Hall College in 1978. She has taught in various parts of the country including East Grinstead, Oxford, and Sheffield. Helena now lives with her husband, who is also half-Polish, in Nottinghamshire where she divides her time between looking after their two children, writing, teaching, and following the trials and tribulations of Huddersfield Town A.F.C. *Simone's Letters* is her second novel for Oxford University Press.

SIMONE'S LETTERS

Helena Pielichaty

Illustrated by Sue Heap

OXFORD
UNIVERSITY PRESS

OXFORD
UNIVERSITY PRESS

Great Clarendon Street, Oxford OX2 6DP

Oxford University Press is a department of the University of Oxford.
It furthers the University's objective of excellence in research, scholarship,
and education by publishing worldwide in

Oxford New York

Athens Auckland Bangkok Bogotá Beunos Aires Calcutta
Cape Town Chennai Dar es Salaam Delhi Florence
Hong Kong Istanbul Karachi Kuala Lumpur Madrid
Melbourne Mexico City Mumbai Nairobi Paris São Paulo
Singapore Taipei Tokyo Toronto Warsaw

with associated companies in
Berlin Ibadan

Oxford is a registered trade mark of Oxford University Press
in the UK and in certain other countries

British Library Cataloguing in Publication Data available

ISBN 0 19 271816 9

Printed and bound in Great Britain by
Biddles Ltd, Guildford and King's Lynn

Dedicated to my mother, Joyce,
with love

MAYHEM THEATRE COMPANY

LONDON—PARIS—HUDDERSFIELD

PRESENTS

RUMPELSTILTSKIN'S REVENGE

THE ROYAL THEATRE BARTOCK

JUNE 30th–JULY 29th

TICKETS FROM BOX OFFICE
ADULTS £4.00
CHILDREN £2.50

HALF PRICE MATINEES FOR PARTIES OF 10 OR MORE

Class Five,
Woodhill Primary School,
Woodhill,
Nr. Bartock.

July 4th

To: Rumpelstiltskin,
    Mayhem Theatre Co.,
    c/o The Royal Theatre,
    Queensgate,
    Bartock.

Dear Rumpelstiltskin,
    I thought the play, *Rumpelstiltskin's Revenge*,
was brilliant. It was the best play I have ever seen. I
liked you the best because you were so funny. My
favourite part was when you did all those cartwheels
and made the straw turn into gold. I thought that
was clever and would like to know this: how did you
change the straw into gold? I never blinked at all and
still can't work out how you did it.
        Yours sincerely,

        Simone Wibberley

        (aged nearly ten)

PS   I was the one who was coughing when King
Coconutty threw his toys all over the floor.

Anthony Bent shoved me in the back when I was eating a Tooty-frooty and it went down the wrong hole. I'm sorry if I made the king forget any of his words.

c/o Royal Theatre,
Queensgate,
Bartock.

July 9th

To: Miss Cassidy and Class,
    Woodhill School,
    Woodhill,
    Nr. Bartock.

Dear Miss Cassidy,
    Thank you and your class very much for your kind letters and drawings. The cast of *Rumpelstiltskin's Revenge* was delighted that you all enjoyed the play so much.
    Unfortunately we are unable to write to everyone individually but your letters will be displayed in the theatre foyer in the near future.
    Meanwhile Mayhem Theatre will be back in Bartock at Christmas with our pantomime, *Cinderella*. We look forward to seeing you all then.
    Yours sincerely,

Jem Cakebread

(Managing Director)

4

Woodhill Primary School,
Woodhill,
Nr. Bartock.

July 14th

Dear Jem Cakebread alias Rumpelstiltskin,
I am writing to you in annoyance and
because I have hay fever and can't do Sports
Day. Miss Cassidy told me to wash the glue
pots out and I've done that so now I'm writing
to you.

clean glue
pots - a
miracle

I'm sort of glad I'm not doing the 60 metres
skipping race because Anthony Bent's in it and he
always wins. I told you about him—he's the one
who made me nearly die on a Tooty-frooty in the
theatre but I couldn't bash him because his mum is a
teacher and was sitting next to him. She said I shouldn't
have been eating in the first place. She's a mardy
teacher. I'll be in her class next year, worst luck.

Miss Cassidy read your letter to us and that's
why I'm writing. No offence, but I don't think it's
fair that you wrote only one letter for everyone.
Miss said I could have a photocopy of the letter if I
was that desperate but I told her it was not the
same. She said it was nice you wrote back at all
and it was hard work in the theatre but I discussed
it with my mum and she said actors didn't know
what hard work was. She said acting was just
grown-ups playing and getting paid for it. I agree
with my mum.

Listen, it took our class three days to write our letters to you. First we had to copy down Miss's words from the board, then finish the sentences in rough then write it up in neat, then do a picture.

It took some of my friends all week. Chloe Madelaine Shepherd had to miss two playtimes because she kept forgetting to put a 'u' in Queensgate in her best copy. Peter Bacon has special needs and rubbed holes in his letter so he had to do it on the computer in the end and that took him and his helper, Mr Cohen, ages, mainly because Mr Cohen couldn't work the computer and kept forgetting to save the text. You should always save the text, in case you didn't know. Mr Cohen is only a student. He has a ponytail. Chloe Madelaine Shepherd is in love with him but it's a secret so don't say anything.

So my letter is a complaint letter really. My mum writes lots of complaint letters. She wrote one to our MP once she was that mad about what he said in the paper about single parents. I think that's why we don't have much money because she uses a lot of stamps.

To summarize, therefore (my mum always writes that near the end of her letters). To summarize, therefore, I think you and the others should have written a letter back to each of us like we did to you. It is only polite. I know you would have had to write the most because you were the most popular but the Queen always writes back and she's much more popular than you, no offence. (I mean Her

Royal Highness Queen Elizabeth II, not Queen Stretchy-Lycra in your play. She was stupid. Only Anthony Bent wrote to her.)

Yours sincerely,

Simone Wibberley

(nearly ten)

PS   I know you were Rumpelstiltskin because your name and photograph were in Miss Cassidy's programme. It says you've been in *The Bill*. I'm not allowed to watch it because it is unsuitable. Chloe Madelaine can but she says she doesn't remember you. Chloe's allowed to watch anything, even films with lots of people snogging, but my mum says that's what happens when kids are given a TV in their bedroom. They end up on a diet of dross.

When I told Chloe Madelaine what my mum had said she went dead mad and said she'd never eaten dross in her life, not even when she went to Tenerife. She didn't sit with me on the swimming bus but she was OK after I gave her my Doritos.

PPS   When you write back, don't forget to tell me about how you changed the straw into gold. I really want to know. I might try it for my next technology project. Technology is my favourite subject. I excel at it, Miss Cassidy says.

Dear Simon,

Thank you for your letter. I'm sorry you feel you and your classmates have been unfairly treated by Mayhem Theatre Company but contrary to your mother's opinion of the acting profession, theatre life is a demanding twenty-four hour job.

In an ideal world we would have time to write to each child but there honestly isn't the time. We had five 'thank you' packages from schools this week alone. If we wrote back to everyone we'd be too tired to go on stage. Unlike the Queen, God bless her, we do not have slaves called Ladies-in-Waiting to reply on our behalf, less popular though we may well be!

I appreciate that all your friends put a great deal of effort into writing our fan mail, although to be quite honest some of the handwriting and spellings make me wonder if you've exaggerated just a tiny bit here. No offence!

Meanwhile, I enclose two complimentary tickets for our next production, *Cinderella*. I hope you and your mother, anti-theatre though she is, will use them to good effect.

Yours etc.

Jem Cakebread

PS   I have actually appeared in *The Bill* twice—

once as a taxi-driver who crashes into a police car and once as a pet-shop owner who is robbed of a valuable parrot. I am also the voice behind Yates's Yummy Yoghurt Bars and Sanderson's Motors of Morley. I do not think my acting is at all 'dross-like' in any shape or form, though I do agree children need more theatre and less TV.

PPS   Don't give your Doritos away to Chloe again. Real friends don't demand packets of crisps.

1 Council House Lane,
Little Woodhill,
Nr. Bartock.

July 22nd

Dear Mr Cakebread,

I am writing back straightaway. For starters my name is Simone, not Simon. I am a girl not a boy. Kids get upset about things like that you know.

I had to show my mum your letter because I couldn't understand it all. She says for someone who's supposed to be running a children's theatre you don't know much about communicating with our age group, although she agreed with you about the Doritos business.

My mum laughed at the bit where you put acting was a twenty-four hour job. She says you want to try cleaning five offices, running a house, going to college, and then getting up in the middle of the night because your daughter (me) is having an asthma attack, then moan because you have to do a couple of cartwheels.

Mum says you sound just like my dad. My dad, Dennis, lives in Bartock with his girlfriend, Alexis. He is thirty-five years old and nearly bald. Alexis is twenty years old, has very long nails and wears tops that show her bra through. My mum says lots of rude things about her because Alexis was one of the reasons my parents got divorced (I was the other). I almost like Alexis now, except she never leaves Dad alone for one minute and I'd like to have some time with him by myself.

Did your parents get a divorce? It's quite common in our school.

Anyway, back to your letter. My mum said it was mean of you to criticize our spellings when you don't know anything about Woodhill. She bets you went to a private school and had a nanny called Lavinia and a pony called Snobby.

Also, I have to send the tickets for *Cinderella* back. In addition to *The Bill*, I'm not allowed to watch anything that makes women out to be brainless hags who treat each other awful and have nothing better to do than wait for a stupid prince to marry. No offence.

Hey, did you know in the real story of Cinderella the glass slipper was really made of fur and the ugly sister cut her toes off with a meat cleaver to make it fit but the prince saw the blood seeping through and knew she wasn't THE ONE. I saw that on television once. Which version are you planning? The glass slipper or the fur slipper?

By the way, my mum is not against the theatre and says when you appear in something more decent than as a parrot seller she might come to watch you.

Yours sincerely,

Simon

(aged ten in seven days)

PS   You still haven't told me how you spun the straw into gold and it's really bugging me. Did someone's hand come through the floor and swap it round?

Bartock

July 27th

Dear Simone,

I'm sorry you have returned the tickets to *Cinderella* so I have sent you two tickets to *Rumpelstiltskin's Revenge* for this Saturday instead. It is the last evening in Bartock so if you don't use the tickets please return them to the box office as they are in much demand. I want you to bring your mother because then she will see:

A)   I do forty-seven cartwheels during the performance. That's forty-seven twice a day, six days a week for fifteen weeks. Get the precious Anthony to work that one out.

B)   Afterwards she can come round the back and watch us 'strike' the set. That means we have two hours in which to take down all the scenery, load it, then clean the theatre. You know how much scenery there was, Simone. It's not like emptying a couple of waste-paper baskets and dusting a cheese plant in some air-conditioned office.

C)   Then we have to drive for miles, in the middle of the night, to our next destination, ready to start all over again.

Theatre life is no picnic! Having said that, I guess your mum doesn't clean offices for the fun of it and bringing up a child on her own can't be easy. Perhaps we've both got hold of the wrong end of the straw!

12

Hope your asthma is better. I had that as a nipper and it's lousy but hopefully you'll grow out of it.

And yes, when you come round to the back of the theatre I will show you how we spun the straw into gold but you mustn't tell anyone. *Rumpelstiltskin's Revenge* runs for another two months yet.

In answer to your other questions and observations:

1.   No, I did not go to private school or have a nanny or a pony called 'Snobby' (as if!). For Ms Wibberley's information I had to pay my own way through Drama School by working nights in a petrol station.

2.   I feel I communicate perfectly well with your age group. If there are any words you do not understand, use a dictionary!

3.   My parents did not get divorced. Sadly my father died when I was six.

Incidentally, for someone not allowed to watch *The Bill* you seem to know an awful lot about blood and mutilation, Simone. Blood seeping from fur slippers? Gruesome!

Anyway, have to dash. Use all your powers of persuasion to get your mum into the theatre— she sounds as if she could do with a break. See you Saturday?

Best wishes,

Jem

1 Council House Lane,
Little Woodhill,
Nr. Bartock.

July 31st

Dear Jem,

I am writing to thank you for the tickets for the play and for showing us round afterwards. It made my birthday really special and miles better than going to the Autojumble which is what my dad had got planned.

It was brilliant coming backstage afterwards. I was nervous about meeting you after what you said about dictionaries but you were cool! You seemed very surprised when you looked at my mum. She's cool, too, isn't she? And your eyes nearly popped out of your head when she did all those cartwheels. I forgot to mention she used to be a fitness instructor before Dad ran off with Alexis. I want her to try out for *Gladiators* but she won't because she's too busy to go round thumping people with a giant cotton bud.

You didn't tell us that in-between 'striking' the set and leaving the theatre actors always have a party. It was weird seeing everyone without their make-up. You danced a lot with my mum and I couldn't help noticing Queen Stretchy-Lycra didn't look very pleased. She wasn't half giving my mum daggers.

Are you married to the Queen in real life? In the foyer it says she is called Sally Smith. That's not a very interesting name for an actor, no offence. I might be an actor when I grow up. I'd be called Paris Dorito and have purple hair.

If you're not married to Sally Smith will you take my mum out? She hasn't had a boyfriend since Dad left and I think it would do her good. I wouldn't ask but you did have the look of love in your eyes, like in the song, when you talked to her. I'm very observant. That's what helps me to excel in technology.

Oh, and guess what? I had a drink of yellow stuff from a paper cup when no one was watching. It tasted disgusting, like drinking cat wee. That was why I was all funny when you were showing me how the straw turned into gold. I felt woozy and the straw kept floating about. I guess I'll never know how it was done. I'll have to think of something else for my technology project.

Don't forget my tip about the slippers being fur instead of glass. You could use ketchup instead of blood.

Yours sincerely,

Simone

(aged ten and proud of it)

PS   Where were all the letters from my school? You said they'd be up in the foyer but they weren't.

August 13th.

Dear Simone,

Thank you for your letter. Glad you enjoyed the party. Say hi to your mum for me. She can dance! I am far too shy to comment on the rest of your letter.

Suffice to say Sally Smith is no longer my queen.

Cheers,

Jem C.

My home no. is: 01384-768881
14, Cruckerne St., Curry Mullet, Exeter

Sorry about the missing letters - maybe they were spun into gold?

Castle Hill, Huddersfield, West Yorkshire
Published by J Hamilton & Co.

S. Wibberley,
1 Council House Lane,
Little Woodhill,
Bartock

1 Council House Lane,
Little Woodhill,
Nr. Bartock.

Aug. 22nd

Hi, Jem,

Hope you are having a great summer holiday. This is a copy of my design for a remote-controlled fur slipper. Feel free to use it in your Christmas panto but don't let any other drama companies get hold of it. I have a feeling it's a winner. R.S.V.P.

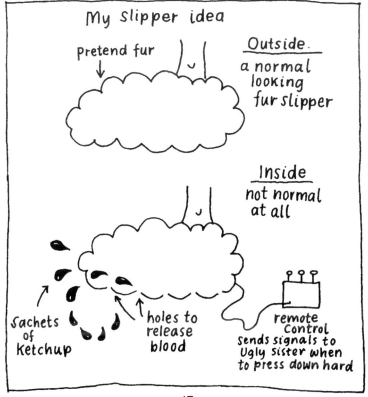

I've not been up to much. All my friends are away on holiday. Peter Bacon lives near me but he's gone to Weymouth and Chloe's gone to Tenerife for more dross. We can't have a holiday this year because Mum has to work all the time but we might zoom off for 'days' soon.

During the holidays I help Mum on cleaning patrol. I like doing the Bramley and Bridlington Building Society best because they have ace twirly seats. They spin round dead fast and make you dizzy. Mum likes doing Mrs Pickering's best because it is the house of her dreams. Every bedroom has a balcony and the kitchen cleans itself, though I don't know how. It's not magic.

When I'm older I'm going to buy Mrs Pickering's house and give it to my mum as a present. That's if Mrs Pickering still owns it. Mum says she's on her last legs and might peg it soon. It must have been sad when your dad died. Did you cry all the time? I would.

This is the second letter I've written today. I wrote to Miss Cassidy as well. She isn't having a holiday this year either because she is house-hunting and she says you can't do both on a teacher's salary. I've been in her class twice; this year and when I was a Year Three. She was really kind when I went through my funny phase. Did I tell you about that? Don't laugh but when Dad left home because of Alexis and me I used to cry every morning and pretend I had gut rot

so I didn't have to go to school. Mum used to bite her lip and say 'Come on, Simone, we've got to get through this,' and push me into the car.

Miss Cassidy would wait by the school gate so Mum could hand me over, screaming and kicking, before she dashed off to work. I was a real pain in the butt but I just couldn't stop. After register, Miss sat with me in the library area when everyone else was in assembly and let me cry and cry. That's dedication, isn't it?

One day she told me that when she was a little girl she used to be scared her dad would be killed in a car crash because whenever their car broke down Mr Cassidy grumbled 'This thing'll be the death of me'. He didn't mean it but like Miss said, when you're young you believe everything an adult tells you. You take things literally, whatever that means.

Anyway, as she had told me something personal I thought it was only fair I should tell her something personal so I told her I was scared my mum would leave me, like Daddy had, and that was why I didn't like coming to school. I figured that if I stayed at home I could watch for danger signs, like notes on the table that said 'I can't cope any more'. I was a real dumbo, but I was only seven nearly eight.

I think Miss Cassidy had a word with my mum because soon after, Mum told me a secret. She always hurried away from the school gate, not because she was fed up with my crying, like I had thought, but because she was crying too. It turned out she was going through a funny phase as well. I stopped crying after that and had to start going to assemblies, worst luck.

Obviously I don't have funny phases any more because I'm ten now. It's a good job, because I have a feeling Mrs Bent doesn't allow them in Year Six. Did you have a funny phase when your dad died?

all the best,

Simone

Our telephone number is Bartock 323211. I did give Mum your telephone number but she nearly fainted when I told her about the look of love. She said you probably had dust in your eye from all that straw and she was quite happy on her own, thank you very much, with a bottle of wine and a Toblerone. I think she's a fibber, though, because I heard her on the phone to my Auntie Laura and she said you were a B-stroke-B plus and even Tom Cruise only gets a B. So, Mum is home all weekend if you are interested. I am spending the weekend with Dad so she might be bored, especially as I know she's definitely already eaten the Toblerone.

14 Cruckerne St.
Curry Mullet
Exeter

Aug. 25th

Dear Simone,
  Tried to get hold of your mum as suggested but the phone was constantly engaged—I was hoping to upgrade my B-stroke-B plus to at least an A minus. Maybe some other time?
  Have passed your fur slipper idea on to Spuddy, my technical adviser (alias King Coconutty in R.R.) who has an eye for these things. We shall certainly consider its merits for Cinderella. Neither of us has had a summer holiday, either, if it's any consolation.
  Yours sincerely,

  a thwarted *Jem Cakebread*.

PS Literally means the exact truth. It's a very misused word—use it sparingly. Are you sure you should be telling me about your funny phases? We have only met once, remember. I don't want you to get into trouble with your mum or dad.

1 Council House Lane,
Little Woodhill,
Woodhill,
Nr. Bartock.

Aug. 30th

Dear Jem,

Thank you for writing back so quickly. Has Spuddy made a decision about my fur slipper design yet? I don't mean to hurry you but I know that Bartock Young Offenders' Centre is literally doing *Cinderella* as well and if you don't want the idea I thought they would, though on second thoughts they might not be allowed meat cleavers for the toe-cutting. Let me know a.s.a.p. anyway, please.

I know why you couldn't get hold of us last weekend. Mum and Dad were arguing on the phone all the time. Like I told you, I was supposed to stay at Dad's on Friday but he forgot to pick me up because Alexis had literally muddled the dates on the calendar. Mum said: 'Well, I suppose I shouldn't be too surprised seeing as it was the twenty-second and she can't count to ten.' Then Dad went mad and Mum hung up. Then she phoned back and he hung up. Then Alexis phoned and Mum made me hang up. My parents are so uncool sometimes. I love them each the same but they tie my feelings into knots when they argue about me. I know it was my fault as much as Alexis's that Dad left in the first place but there's no need for them to keep going on and on rowing over me. I hate it. They don't have the look of love when they talk. Not one blink. Literally.

In the end I just went to Chloe's. She is back from Tenerife. She brought me a teddy that said 'I flew Arrow Airlines' across its chest. He's sweet and I have called him Cakebread after you. Chloe and me discussed action plans for dealing with Mrs Bent when we start back next week. We called it 'New Term, New Tortures' then we wrote our wills. I would have liked to have done something else but like Chloe said, her house equals her rules.

Today I looked up 'thwarted' in my dictionary. I literally like the word 'thwarted'. The dictionary said: *say 'thwort' verb: to prevent something being done successfully: 'the police thwarted the attempted bank robbery.'* I've been saying it all day to Mum. She's promised me she'll ring you if I stop. I'd like to meet you again because you are funny and quite good-looking without your make-up. Oh, and you don't have to worry about what you write to me, by the way. I keep all your letters in a Lion's wine gum box with 'private' written on it. I know my mum won't read your letters because she's not like that, so if there's anything you want to tell me, like how your dad died and was it painful, feel free.

Don't forget the fur slipper design.

Yours thwortfully,

Simone

Dear Simone,

I am sending you my best wishes on this giant postcard of Birmingham Town Hall. I'm waiting in a cold studio to audition for a voice-over in a radio commercial for Squeezy-Cheeze. 'Kids'll say please for Squeezy-Cheeze.' Yeah, sure they will.

First of all, I am overwhelmed to have a teddy bear named after me. Congratulations on your fine taste.

Next. The good news is, Spuddy reckons we should give your fur slipper a go! He'll have to make some adjustments to your design but we've got plenty of time to work on it.

I'm sorry your parents got your visiting days mixed up—you must feel like piggy-in-the-middle sometimes but you know it's not really any of my bees-knees. I try to keep out of family affairs as these things can get complicated, private wine gum box or no private wine gum box. At the risk of contradicting myself, however, what do you mean when you say it's your fault your parents split up? That's nonsense. Children aren't to blame when their parents divorce or are unhappy, honestly. It seems to me you need another talk with Miss Cassidy.

And where were you when I finally plucked up courage to call your house? Round at Peter Bacon's I heard. Do we have a 'look of love'

S. Wibberley,
1 Council House Lane,
Little Woodhill,
Bartock

situation here? Or is it mean to tease? What do
you think about your mum agreeing to come out
with me next week? Any tips? Should I bring
flowers or Toblerone or Squeezy-Cheeze?

Hey—I'm a poet and didn't know it! Good luck
at school.

Jem xx

PS   You know I told you to use the word
'literally' sparingly? Look up the word
'sparingly'!

The Usual Place
Wittle Hoodhill,
Hoodhill,
Nr. Tarbock.

Sept. 7th

Hi Jem,

I am really, really pleased my fur slipper design is being used in *Cinderella*. Even Mrs Bent was impressed and gave me a 'Well Done' stamp. I would have preferred a 'Super Work' sticker but they only go to outstanding pieces and her precious son Anthony. She uses them sparingly. Mrs Bent has booked our class to see *Cinderella* on December 13th because the seats were all half price that day and she said she'd better get in quick. We have only been back a week and already we are having to save money and think about secondary school.

Now for the important part. I have written a list of tips for you on how to have a good time with my mum. She is already excited. Here goes:

1. Chocolates are a very good idea. She likes Elizabeth Swigg's Mint Crisps best—I buy her those every Christmas. If you're poor, Toblerones are her second favourite. We've never had Squeezy-Cheeze so I can't comment on that suggestion.

2. If you go to McDonald's ask them to take the gherkins out first.

3. She tells you off if you slurp your drinks and chew your ice cubes noisily.

4.   If she has a pudding don't say,
'Are you sure you want that? You'll get
fat.' Dad used to do that. She goes red
in the face then throws the pudding at you.
Watch it because rhubarb crumble can burn.

5.   Names. She is called Cathryn. Don't use
Caff, Caffy, Babe, or worst of all, Alexis. Dad used
to call her all those and it led to big trouble.

6.   Please go somewhere cheap to eat. She'll insist
on paying half and we've only got one Family
Allowance due. I wouldn't go to the Bartock Balti
because Dad always takes Alexis there and it might
end up in a fight.

Hope these tips are useful.

Simone Wibberley Designs Inc.

PS   I did make my parents split up, Jem, but it was
an accident. I kept having asthma attacks so Mum
couldn't go to work and we didn't have enough
money and that made them argue. After an argument
Dad would go to the pub and not come in until late,
then they would argue again and I would get another
asthma attack. If I didn't have asthma, Dad would
never have gone to The Bag O' Nuts Fun Pub and
met Alexis and left an 'I can't cope' note on the
kitchen table. There's no use seeing Miss Cassidy
because it's the truth and the truth is the truth.
Literally, not sparingly.

14 Cruckerne St.,
Curry Mullet,
Nr. Exeter.

14th Sept.

Dear Simone,
   Just a quick 'thank you' for the tips you gave me. They were very useful and I managed to escape either being pelted with rhubarb crumble or boxing with your dad, so the meal must have been a success. You probably know we talked about you most of the evening, though we did throw in the odd sentence about books, politics, music, and education. I found out your middle name is Anna and you weighed six pounds eleven ounces when you were born and that you once cut all your hair off in an experiment with left-handed scissors. Remind me not to fall asleep anywhere near you! See you soon, I hope.
   Let me know if I reached an A minus with my smooth-talking ways.
      Best wishes,

   Jem xx

1 Council House Lane,
Little Woodhill,
Nr. Bartock.

Sept. 16th

Dear Jem,

I am glad you had a good time with Mum. She didn't mention a grade but told me you made her laugh which is a miracle seeing as you talked about such boring stuff—apart from the bits about me, of course. Laughing's very important. Alexis and I did a questionnaire in one of her magazines on true love and it said being able to laugh with your partner was vital in a relationship. I asked Alexis if Dad made her laugh and she said yes, when he took his clothes off. No comment.

Did you tell Mum about me knowing the divorce was my fault? I think you did because she let me stay up late to have a 'girls' talk' last night. We had hot chocolate with marshmallows, biscuits and the gas fire on 'full'—the whole caboodle.

She said the same as you said in your other letter, that Daddy leaving home had nothing to do with me or my asthma and that things had been going wrong for a long time, even before I was born. Mum explained that sometimes people fall out of love and it's nobody's fault, it just happens. She was upset that I had thought it was my fault and we both had a little cry like when we were going through our funny phase. She said I had to tell her next time I was worried about anything and it was healthier to get stuff off your chest. Then we finished the biscuits.

I feel a bit better now that I know the divorce wasn't my fault but there's still something bugging me. Why couldn't Dad stay anyway, to be with me? They could have put a curtain down the middle of their bedroom like Peter Bacon and his brother have got to stop them fighting. And they could have had a rota for the TV like we have at school for the computer. It would save me a lot of travelling at weekends and them money on two of everything. You're lucky your parents never divorced but unlucky your dad died. Which do you think is worse?

You ended your letter 'see you soon'. Do you mean it? Mum says you are going to the Midlands to show *Rumpelstiltskin's Revenge* and won't be back for weeks. When can you come to our house for tea? I'll make you chocolate chip cookies.

See you soon,

Simone x

Mrs Gupta's Guest House,
Wolverhampton

Sept. 30th

Dear Simone,

I'm so glad you have sorted everything out with Cathryn about the divorce. You take after your mother, who is very sensible, as well as beautiful.

Well, we finally arrived in Wolverhampton after spending the night on the hard shoulder of the motorway because Spuddy's clapped out old van clapped out totally. Usually we travel in Sal's car but she hasn't spoken to me since our final performance in Bartock. If you came to see *Rumpelstiltskin's Revenge* here you would notice a few unscripted changes where Queen Stretchy-Lycra hits me on the head with a rubber brick and tries to trip me up during my somersaulting. I told you theatre life was no picnic!

How's school going? Is Anthony behaving himself? Is Chloe still bossing you around? She does boss you around, you know! She'd make a good Princess Stretchy-Lycra.

I'll definitely be there for tea.

Best wishes,

Jem

You know the address

Oct. 2nd

Dear Jem,

I'm sorry Queen Stretchy is being mean but she does have a broken heart and that takes a while to heal, maybe six to eight days. Perhaps you could ask Spuddy to fall in love with her instead and then everyone will be happy. Only don't let it distract him from designing the slipper. How far has he got? Anthony Bent doesn't believe you will go through with it, big pain in the neck that he is.

I know Chloe's bossy sometimes but that's just her way. She has good points, too, like letting me borrow her felt pens if mine run out and always being my partner in country dancing. I was a bit sad when she asked for Cakebread back, though; I admit it. You see, he was supposed to be a holiday swap but because I didn't go on holiday I had nothing to swap him with so I had to return him. Dad let me choose anything I wanted from the shop instead but you can't cuddle a bag of liquorice lumps. Oh, well, hasta la blister, baby!

I can't wait to see you.

Love, Simone XXX

Wolverhampton

Oct. 9th

Dear Simone,

I am so, so sorry I couldn't get to your house for tea on Thursday. As I explained to Cathryn on the phone, Sal had booked an extra matinee performance at All Saints Primary without bothering to tell the rest of us. There was no way I would have made it to Bartock and back for the next day and it was too late to cancel, even if we could afford to. Mind you, if ever a school were mis-named, it was that one. All Brats more like it. Even the infants had tattoos!

Anyway, I'm sorry again, Simone. I was disappointed too as I was looking forward to the cookies. I hope this little gift makes up for it.

Humble apologies,

Jem xxxx

1 Council House Lane,
Little Woodhill,
Nr. Bartock.

October 13th

Dear Mr Cakebread,
   You don't have to apologize to me. I know I'm
only a kid and not as important as infants with
tattoos. Mum tried to make excuses for you about
theatre life and sounded like Miss Cassidy did when I
first complained about you not writing back.
   Thank you for the zebra. He's OK but not as cute
as Cakebread. No offence, but you remind me of my
dad. Every time he forgets to collect me for custardy
time he sends me a present. He doesn't understand
that I'd rather see him than have more toys, either.
   Yours sincerely,

Simone Anna Wibberley

PS   No need to worry about the cookies. We put
them in the freezer for 'Trick or Treat' night, ready
for distribution to the needy.

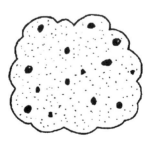

'The Tea Kettle' B&B
Birmingham

October 20th

Dear Simone,

This is a difficult letter to write. I realize from your short reply and from what Cathryn tells me when I telephone that you are hurt that I let you down. Well, I've already apologized—what more can I say? I am an actor with a travelling theatre group. That's my job. Sometimes I don't get any work for months so when I get the chance I have to grab it, just like your mum does with her cleaning. If we are going to be friends it means you won't see much of me and often I will cancel things at the last minute, but I will write whenever I can.

Maybe the zebra was a mistake, although I sent him to replace Cakebread because I thought Chloe was rotten for asking for her gift back, not because I felt guilty. Give him away if you don't want to keep him.

To tell you the truth, I'm a bit peeved at being compared to your father. Blimey! Hit me with a rubber brick if I'm wrong but I hardly think a friend postponing tea because he has to work is on the same lines as leaving your family to set up a shop with another woman. All I can say is, if I were a father, I would try not to let my children down like yours and mine did.

The thing is, Simone, I lied to you about my father dying. He just walked out on us when I was six and never came back. We didn't have the cold comfort of an 'I can't cope' note—no explanation—nothing. Even now I feel very angry towards him which is why I tell everyone he is dead. Not even Spuddy knows the truth.

So, while your dad might get times and dates mixed up occasionally, at least you do see him. More importantly, when you are older, he'll be there to answer your questions about why he left. I'll never know why mine did.

Fondest regards,

Jem

1 Council House Lane,
Little Woodhill,
Bartock

October 29th

Dear Jem,

Thank you for your letter. You'll be glad to know I've hidden it right at the bottom of my wine gum box, right underneath the wax paper so no one will ever know your secret about your ✳✳✳. I can keep a secret really well. I've kept a secret about what Peter Bacon did with his brother Luther's gerbil for two and a half years now, so you can trust me. Just remember, it wasn't your fault your ✳✳✳ left. You taught me that.

Zebra is now called Spotty. Get it—Spotty—when it's a zebra? There's no way I'll ever give him away. Chloe's green as mushy peas. She wanted me to have Cakebread back in exchange but I said 'Not on your nellie, smelly'. She sat with Kayleigh, Emma, Harry, and the two Joes at lunchtime but I didn't care. I helped Miss Cassidy weed the Wildlife Garden. Mum says I'm getting to be a tough cookie in my old age and she's proud of me. That reminded me of the biscuits still in the freezer. I asked Mum if we could leave them there until you came instead of giving them away on Hallowe'en. She said OK and smiled.

Dad gave me a heap of sweets from the penny mix section instead, though he looked peeved when I told him why. He keeps asking me about you. I think he's got the green-eyed monster. That is not good for a relationship. Nothing kills a relationship faster than the green-eyed monster according to Alexis's latest magazine but like Mum says, who we give our cookies to is none of his beeswax.

I hope you notice how I always use the new words you teach me? I like peeved better than literally but not as much as thwarted. I used thwarted in my creative writing today and Mrs Bent said it was a very good choice of word for a Year Six pupil. She is always telling us to expand our vocabulary ready for secondary school. I'll be going to Bartock High. Dad says the kids from Bartock High come in his shop and their vocabulary has expanded too far already for his liking.

Best wishes,

Nov. 9th

Hathaway House B&B
Stratford

28P

CRACK THE CODE SIMONE

1 = C	2 = D	3 = E	4 = F	5 = H
6 = I	7 = K	8 = O	9 = R	10 = S
11 = T				

2 3 4 9 8 10 11   11 5 3   1 8 8 7 6 3 10

Jem xx

PS   We have business to discuss

S. Wibberley,
1 Council House Lane,
Little Woodhill,
Bartock

39

1 Council House Lane,
Little Woodhill,
Nr Bartock

November 15th

Dear Jem,
    It was great to see you when you and Spuddy came
to tea. Sorry if the cookies were a bit stale but you
never said in your code exactly when you were
coming. They tasted all right dipped in hot fudge
sauce though, didn't they?
    Now down to business. As you know, Spuddy has
made me his Junior Design Consultant for Footwear.
He asked me to choose the fabric for the Ugly Sisters'
slippers. After much thought I have chosen fabric A.
Fabric A is lighter than the others and so will show the
blood more when it seeps through. Please pass on my
decision to Spuddy as soon as you can. I want him to
know I can meet a deadline.
    I think *Cinderella* will be cool. I can't wait to see you
as Fairy Gobmother. Mum has booked tickets for
Christmas Eve so I'll see you twice! She says she's had a
change of heart about the women in the play now that
you explained Mayhem's version of the script to her. Is
that why you spent ages and ages in the kitchen? It
must be a long script. Should I take a cushion when I
go to the theatre?
    I noticed the look of love was still there. Spuddy
says you're smitten. I'm sorry to have to tell you this
but I like the word 'smitten' better than 'thwarted'. It

means to hit hard. I was worried at first because I thought you were going to hit my mum and I'd have to do some karate on you but then I realized it means that love has hit you hard.

I told Dad you were smitten with Mum and he frowned. He's not very good with long words. I don't think they did vocabulary extension when he was at school.

Won't it be funny if I have to write another 'thank you' letter after our school trip on December 13th? I bet we do—it's tradition. I won't mention being Junior Design Consultant in my letter though because the others might think I'm getting too big for my boots. Or slippers. Ha-Ha!

Simone Wibberley

J.D.C. (footwear)

Class Six,
Woodhill Primary School,
Woodhill,
Nr. Bartock.

December 19th

To: Fairy Gobmother,
     Mayhem Theatre Co.,
     c/o The Royal Theatre,
     Queensgate,
     Bartock.

Dear Fairy Gobmother,
    I thought the pantomime, *Cinderella*, was
fantastic. It was nearly as good as *Rumpelstiltskin's
Revenge*. I liked you best because you were so funny.
My favourite part was when your bloomers kept
falling down, even though I found out later they
weren't supposed to. I also thought having a fur
slipper instead of the boring old glass slipper was a
stroke of genius and very effective. I hope you write
back to us all this time.
    Yours sincerely,

    Simone Wibberley.

PS   I'm adding this bit in secret. Mrs Simpson, the
secretary, is letting me. Mrs Bent says we aren't
allowed to put personal messages or put that the best
bit was when Anthony got splurged with ketchup,

even though it was, but I don't care. It serves him right for pushing to the front of the stage when the Ugly Sister was sawing her toes off. He went: 'This won't work in a million years, Dribberley-Wibberley,' then the sauce squirted all over him. I know Mrs Bent made you pay for the dry-cleaning. Told you she was mardy. You should have taken it to Chloe's dad's shop on the High Street. He might have done it for half-price if you had told him you were a friend of the family.

When you come to our house again tomorrow I want to give you my improved design for the fur slipper, in case you do *Cinderella* again next year. I bought these rubber toes which I thought would look brilliant flying through the air after the Ugly Sister had chopped them off. They're rounded at the end so they won't hurt anyone.

love, Simone X X X X X

 Mayhem Theatre Company

Jan. 4th

Dear Mrs Bent and pupils of Class Six,

Thank you and your class very much for the kind letters and drawings. The cast of *Cinderella* was delighted that you all enjoyed the play so much.

Unfortunately we are unable to write to everyone individually but your letters will be displayed in the theatre foyer in the near future. I understand this did not occur after *Rumpelstiltskin's Revenge* but can assure you that I will personally mount the work this time. We were particularly impressed by Peter Bacon's drawing of the Ugly Sisters, though I don't remember them actually using hand grenades and machine guns, Peter.

I do hope Anthony's suit is as good as new. We do try to encourage the audience to remain in their seats unless invited on to stage so that such mishaps do not occur. I respectfully suggest Anthony remembers this in future.

Hopefully Mayhem Theatre Company will see you all in June when we are bringing Lionel Bart's smash hit musical *Oliver!* to Bartock.

Very best wishes,

Jem Cakebread

(Managing Director)

Dear Simone,

Just a quick note from Spuddy's bed-sit. We're going through the script for *Oliver!* before heading north to take my gear to my mum's. I expect Cathryn told you about Sal evicting me from my room in favour of a biology student from Swansea? Charming! I bet you any money he won't clean the grill pan out after making cheese toasties like I did!

I'm really grateful to you and your mum for allowing me to stay in your spare room when we are touring round Bartock but promise not to laugh at my Spiderman pyjamas; they were a present from an aunt who thinks I'm still twelve!

I have a big favour to ask. You know the letters from your school? I left them somewhere in the theatre but can't remember where. If you're passing, could you drop in and enquire about them? I don't want Mrs Bent falling out with me, especially as we rely on kind, sweet teachers like her to bring lovely, well-behaved children like you to our performances. Creep! Creep! If you do find them, you could help me to put them on display at the weekend while your mum finishes her essay for college.

Meanwhile, Spuddy says if you have any suggestions for *Oliver!* such as how we put on a show designed for a minimum of thirty actors with five of us and a dog called Mary, he will be forever in your debt.

Lots of love,

Jem xxx

MAYHEM THEATRE COMPANY

LONDON—PARIS—HUDDERSFIELD

PRESENTS

LIONEL BART'S

OLIVER!

THE ROYAL THEATRE
BARTOCK

JUNE 8th–JUNE 12th

TICKETS FROM BOX OFFICE
ADULTS £5.50
CHILDREN £3.00

HALF PRICE MATINEES FOR PARTIES OF 10 OR MORE

sorry forgot

1 Council House Lane,
Little Woodhill,
Nr Bartock,
Nr. Europe,
The World,
Earth.

April 5th

Dear Chlo Deline,

Thanks for your postcard of Sidney's Opera House. It's the first card I've had in ages. Jem used to write but he just about lives with us now so I only get mail occasionally, unless you count Post-its from my mum saying 'Tidy this mess NOW!!'

You are so jammy getting two months off school to visit your gran in Australia, even if she does wear leather jackets and ride a motor bike. I don't agree with your dad that she's potty. I think she sounds cool.

You're not missing anything in class. Mrs Bent is as boring as ever and picks on me all the time. As we all know she's still got it in for me since *Cinderella* and the tomato sauce business.

Example: yesterday I asked her if we could go to see *Oliver!* when it comes to the Royal Theatre in June and she went, 'No, because we're not doing the Victorians and besides, the Mayhem Theatre Company has a poor reputation for losing children's work.' She said it really loud in front of everybody. I told her it wasn't Jem's fault the cleaners at the theatre threw out our work about *Cinderella* but she wouldn't listen. I think she's just jealous that my mum's boyfriend is a Potentially Famous Actor while her husband is a Dumb Computer Programmer.

Guess which topic we are doing this term? Local Study. For about the fiftieth time. Benty says if I have a complaint about the National Curriculum I should write to the government—as if they would know anything. Meanwhile, I've got the joy of writing to my own dad and asking him to fill in a questionnaire about shops and trade in Bartock. Wow.

Of course, Mrs Bent wouldn't let me write to the new Dream-ee Toffee factory on Yeovil Road instead, would she? That pleasure went to her little boy Anthony. What a waste. Everyone knows he's not allowed even to sniff a toffee in case his teeth turn black and drop out one second later. I would have asked for samples and everything.

It's not the same without you. Melanie McCleod's got your tray now. She's been moved out of Miss Cassidy's because Miss couldn't control her. Melanie read your postcard at break without asking and said she thought Deline was a pathetic name to call yourself and Chloe was better, though not much better. I told her we all have a right to call ourselves whatever we wanted and that Deline was only your holiday name so she said to me, 'What's yours then? Moaner?' As if that was even slightly funny or one bit original. I think Melanie McCleod's a right c-o-double-u.

Speaking of names, Mum says I'm old enough to call her Cathryn. She said it's more up-beat. She's changed a lot since Valentine's Day when Jem asked her out properly and she gave him an A minus. He wanted an A but as Mum says, nobody's perfect.

It's as if her and Dad have swapped round now. When Dad first left to live above the 'News Shack' with Alexis he was the one always cracking jokes and buying me stuff while Mum cried all day. Now he just grunts while Mum sings about jelly and custard.

Fridays are the worst when she's waiting for Jem to arrive for the weekend if he's been working away. She goes through every song from *Oliver!*—even the slow ones—every verse. It's like living with Celine Dion. (Hey: Celine rhymes with Deline!) I bet Mum'll be really fed up when *Oliver!* starts properly and Jem can only visit on Sundays. Come to think of it, so will I. He's taught me how to use a fretsaw and never says 'in a minute' when he means 'in a year'. I never feel like piggy-in-the-middle when he and Mum are together. I like him loads.

Meanwhile, Dad's not gone 'up-beat' at all; when I tried to call him Dennis he nearly bit my head off. He's been really mardy lately. Maybe it's because Alexis has lost her looks. She doesn't wear see-through crop-tops any more and is always throwing up when I visit.

Got to go now. Mrs Bent wants our draft copies of the Local Study questionnaires in by tomorrow so I'd better get on with it. Did you know teachers can't actually force you to do homework? It's not the law but Mum says it's good practice for secondary school so I have to do it. Pity she's not gone as up-beat about education as she has about names. Oh well.

Love from your number one best friend,

Simone xxxxxxx x xx xx xx x xx x x xxx X

Dear Deline,

I know you won't have got my first letter yet but I wanted to write to you straight away with my new news. Guess what? Dad and Alexis are going to get married and I'm going to be a bridesmaid, even if Mum does think it will be a sham. When I asked her what a sham was she said 'look it up' but I didn't understand my dictionary. It said: *A pretence: 'his illness was only a sham'*. That doesn't make sense— you can't pretend to get married. You have to have witnesses who can witness against you. Maybe she meant 'a shame'.

Anyway, the wedding's in four weeks and I can invite a friend. I know you won't be able to come but I'm sending you an invitation anyway. Alexis let me tear one off her pad. She looked a lot better yesterday and has started wearing her false nails again. Maybe she was being sick because of pre-wedding nerves. This can happen, according to *Wedded Bliss*, one of the million bride's magazines she's bought. Dad says he'll be bankrupt before the year's out.

Dad even *apologized* for being snappy lately but said getting married again was a big surprise to him as well as me. I think he's used to the idea now. He let me stick an *Oliver!* poster up in his window, hardly blinking at all when he saw it was for the Mayhem Theatre Company. I have the feeling he doesn't like culture much. Mum told me the last time

Dad set foot in a theatre he was wearing a cowboy hat and shouting 'Crackerjack'. *Crackerjack* was a kid's TV programme from the olden days. Guess what the prizes were if you won? Pencils. No wonder he never went back.

The bad news about the wedding is that Melanie McCleod will be there. Her oldest sister, Toni, is Alexis's best friend and Melanie has to be there to look after Toni's baby, Conan, so Toni can relax and be a proper Matron of Honour. I'm still excited, though.

Love, *Simone*

Your number one best friend

PS   I nearly forgot to tell you. The Dream-ee Toffee factory faxed Anthony and have invited the whole class to look round the week after next. Mega. Wish you were here to be my partner.

Wedding Invitation

Alexis & Dennis

cordially invite

Chloe Madelaine Shepherd

to attend their wedding ceremony

at: Bartock Registry Office

on: Sat. May 7th 11.00 a.m.

Reception afterwards at

The Jug & Frog pub

RSVP
The News Shack
45 High Street
Bartock

'Bally-Hi'
Harbour Ridge,
Sydney
Australia.

April 12th

Dear Simone,
    Both your letters arrived today.
    I've only been out of the country for two weeks
and I'm already being victimized. I cannot believe
Melanie McCleod has got my tray. Why, why, oh why,
did you let her take it? You could have hidden it in
the paint cupboard or something until I got back. If
she'd have tried to get your tray I'd have told. And I
left my Man. U. pencil case in it. Who's got that?
Melanie McCleod I suppose. She's more than a c-o-
double-u, she's a dag. A dag is Australian for
something really disgusting. I still cannot believe you
did nothing to save my tray. What sort of a friend
are you?
    Mummy's sent a letter to give to Mrs Bent. Make
sure you pass it on straight away. Mummy said if it
wasn't for the fact I'm a Y6 she'd send me to a private
school. She says I'm not being pushed enough at
Woodhill.
    Thanks but no thanks for the invitation to your
dad's wedding but even if I was in Bartock I
wouldn't have been able to go to it. Mummy says
the Jug and Frog has a bad reputation and only
students and people from rough housing estates
drink there.
    By the way, if Melanie McCleod reads this letter, I

won't bother writing again. Private means private in my book.

Yours faithfully,

C. M. Shepherd (I have outgrown Deline)

PS   Has it never occurred to you that some people might not be interested in what your mum's boyfriend is up to? Being an actor is nothing special, you know. Like I told you before, it's not life-saving. I think my daddy's job as manager of two dry-cleaning shops is much more important. At least our clothes are never creased and we have thousands of coat hangers.

1 Council House Lane,
Little Woodhill,
Nr Bartock.

April 24th

Dear C. M. Shepherd,
   Sorry it has taken me so long to reply but I have
been very poorly and not felt like doing much. I had
an asthma attack when we were on the school trip to
the toffee factory. Lucky for me Melanie was my
partner and just about saved my life. She found my
inhaler when I couldn't breathe properly and ran for
help when the inhaler didn't make any difference.
Mrs Bent called for an ambulance and I was carried
out of the factory on a stretcher and all the toffee
machines stopped working. It was so cool.
   Melanie came with me to the hospital and stayed
until Mum and Dad and Alexis arrived. Jem was in
Taunton so he couldn't come. I had to stay in hospital
overnight but was OK enough to go home the next day.
Anyway, this letter from Anthony gives all the details.
Please send it back when you have finished with it.
   Back to your letter. I'm sorry you don't think I'm a
very good friend for not saving your tray. I'm sure
you'll get it back when your holiday ends. If not you
can have mine and I'll share with Mel—she's not
that bad when you get to know her, especially during
an emergency.

Love from Simone xxxxxx x xx

April 23rd AD

To: Miss S. Wibberley,
    1 Council House Lane,
    Little Woodhill,
    Bartock.

Dear Simone W.,

I am writing to request your forgiveness with regards to the unfortunate incident which occurred in the Dream-ee Toffee factory on Monday, April 19th at approximately 11.23 a.m.

I deeply regret that you had an asthma attack as a result of my actions but if I might be permitted to put forward my view of the incident you might look upon things a bit differently. Then, once you are feeling better, you might want to write to our class and persuade them to stop throwing my packed lunch into the Wildlife Garden which, as you know, is out of bounds, even to children of senior staff members.

Melanie McC. has been especially belligerent towards me. As she isn't pleasant on a normal day, owing to her background, you can imagine what an effect her negative attitude is having on my learning process. I am being groomed for the scholarship exam to Alabaster Boys, you know.

But back to that fateful trip. As you remember, mother had repeatedly told the whole class to walk down the aisles in pairs. My partner Harry B. and I were the leaders. (You may recall saying 'Huh, typical' rather spitefully when mother announced this but I was the one who organized the whole trip in the first place, and besides, I do have leadership qualities). Unfortunately, Harry is a slow walker and for some reason kept falling behind and trying to make a three with Joe P. and Freddie J. and you know what the rule on threes is.

This continued up the Russian caramel aisle, along the penny chew section and throughout the whole length of the liquorice lumps. I hardly had a chance to make any notes at all. By the time we reached the bon-bon section I was pretty frazzled with having to drag Harry back to the front every two minutes. I would have told mother but she was still taking photographs of the Russian caramels and the parent helpers were too busy chatting about sweets they used to eat as children to listen to my protests.

We had just reached the lime bon-bon machine when Harry tried to escape again. In my desperation to hold on to him and our leadership position I reached out my arm to secure his sweatshirt. I swear on my mother's Mark Book I didn't see you leaning over the machine just as my arm missed Harry and swung into your back, knocking you into the freshly opened sacks of icing sugar next to us. I realize how this would have been upsetting for even a normal child, but for one prone to asthma and hay fever it could have been fatal. Fortunately for me, it wasn't.

I put it to you, therefore, that this whole sorry incident was really Harry B.'s fault and it's his sandwiches which should be in the Wildlife Garden every lunchtime and not mine.

I would also like to add that my mother had nothing to do with the writing of this letter.
Pax?
Your fellow colleague,

Anthony Beaumont Bent

1 Council House Lane,
Little Woodhill,
Nr. Bartock.

May 1st

Dear Chloe,

Thanks for your telephone call which woke my mum at 3.00 this morning even though you'd already had your lunch. I still don't get how that time zone thing works. Mrs Bent told us that when it's Christmas, Australians are having their summer and they eat turkey on the beach. Can you find out if that's true?

Yes, I am much better. Like I said, I had to stay one night in hospital; it was one of the worst attacks I've had but it seems like ages ago now. I'm sorry if you were all worried. My mum said your mum said it made you realize what a good friend I was to you and to forget all about the silly tray business, you were just missing me and felt left out. I'm missing you, too!

To answer your other questions which Mum wrote down for me:

1.   Yes, I do hang out with Melanie McCleod now: she is my first equal best friend along with you. After all, she did save my life. I hope we can all be friends.

2.   No, I can't sit with you when you return—not even on the swimming bus. That's not because I'm sitting next to Melanie but because Mrs Bent is making us sit boy-girl-boy-girl. I think she's flipped. My partner is Peter Bacon. No comment.

3.   Yes, it is too late to fly back for the wedding as there is not going to be a wedding. It turned out Alexis and Dad were only going to get married because Alexis thought she was going to have a baby! I was shocked at first, literally, then just as I was getting used to the idea and planning names, Alexis decided not to have a baby any more and had a false alarm instead.

Dad said there was no point getting married then and cancelled everything except the party at the Jug and Frog. Alexis hasn't stopped crying yet but Mum says she'll be grateful in the end because Dennis Wibberley was not cut out to be husband material. I'm very sad because I like the idea of having a baby brother or sister even if their dirty nappies smell worse than bad bananas stuck down a tramp's underpants like Mel says.

Something else strange happened soon after. I was helping Dad put out the new cards which had arrived for Father's Day when I said to him, 'Dad, you know if Alexis did have a baby instead of a false alarm, would you leave an "I can't cope" note for Alexis and the baby when the baby was seven nearly eight or would you just not leave anything this time?'

He asked what I meant and when I explained, do you know what he did? He started crying! Honest. Not those big, wet tears that make your nose run but small pools of tears that gather round the bottom of the eyes like a miniature duck pond. He gave me a tight hug that bent two of the cards I was carrying and said, 'I'm sorry, petal, I'm sorry. I wish I'd had the guts to be more honest with you at the time but I thought you were too young to understand.' Too young! As if! Grown-ups haven't got the faintest sometimes, have they?

I wanted to cry a bit myself but I don't have funny phases any more so I held back. Dad's hug made me feel sad-happy but most important of all I know he loves me and always has and always will, even if he is an unreliable waste of space (Mum's words not mine). Does your dad ever cry?

Anyway, I'm looking forward to seeing you when you return. Melanie is fun but we don't go way back to nursery school like you and me. By the way, Jem says he'll be happy to push you if that's what your parents still want.

Simone.

................................—you fill this bit in

'Bally-Hi',
Harbour Ridge,
Sydney
Australia

May 12th

Dear Simone,
I got your letter about everything. You sound very busy, even if the wedding has been called off. Mummy said it was probably a blessing in disguise. I'm not sure what this means—Jem will probably explain. Mummy asked me to ask you if he was planning to marry Cathryn, to set a good example to you. Let me know. I did ask about time-zones but it's complicated—Gran says she's going to find you a book about it. She thinks you are a smart kid. I told her I was ahead of you in Zig-zag maths but behind you in technology.
You sound as if you are having a great time with M.McC. I'm sorry, Simone, but I don't know what you see in her, even if she did run for the ambulance. You do realize that if I had been your partner I would have done exactly the same, only quicker, probably.
Simone, you may be shocked by what I have to say next so fetch your inhaler before you read on, just in case. I think you should know that the McCleods are of the criminal classes. As you know, Mummy used to be a secretary at Bartock Magistrates Court and she said if there wasn't one McCleod up in front of the bench it was another. LeeRoy McCleod was the worst, so go home immediately if he drops in if you're ever round M's house. I wouldn't go to her house for tea

anyway. I can't imagine the food would be very good or hygienic. Not like at mine.

I asked Mummy if we could come back on an earlier flight so I can rescue you from bad company but the answer was no and not to ask again. They don't care that everything is changing and dropping to bits in England and I'm not there to stop it. It's all right for them. They have made friends with Mr and Mrs Ling who own most of the dry-cleaning shops round here. They spend every day touring the malls and comparing chemicals and coat hangers. I have to go with them because Gran refuses to babysit for me every day. She told them they'd come to the wrong house for Mary Poppins. I could go with her to the horse racing if I wanted but I'm not allowed to ride on the back of her motorbike.

You might think your father is weird for crying but that's nothing compared to my grandmother; she dyes her hair blonde and has three boyfriends in one go! Daddy says she's had too much sun and it's sent her barmy but Gran just laughs and says she's planning on growing old disgracefully before she turns out to be an old fart like him. If I'd said that to Daddy I'd be grounded for life. Her language is a disgrace for a woman of nearly sixty with a hearing impairment.

As a gesture of goodwill, I'm sending Moony to you, or Cakebread as you called him, special delivery, so it should reach you soon. That shows what a nice best friend I am, doesn't it?

Best wishes, Simone, old pal.

Chloe Shepherd xxxxxxx x xx xx

x xxxxxxx x xx xx xx x xxx x x x xxx

I flew
Arrow
airlines

65

1 Council House Lane,
Little Woodhill,
Nr. Bartock.

May 19th

Dear Chloe,

I really enjoyed hearing from you, though I haven't received Cakebread yet, or Anthony's letter, come to think of it. There's loads to tell you so I've divided this letter up into subjects but before I do, can I ask you one thing? Can you stop being nasty about Melanie? It's not her fault she comes from a family with a bad reputation or that her dad's in jail. I only found that out myself yesterday. I knew he didn't live at her house but when I asked her if he had left a note before going she said he didn't have time, what with trying to hide three satellite dishes under the table before the police broke the door down.

He writes poems to her every week from prison. That shows he's a caring person. Also, the food at her house is brilliant. We have fish finger and Squeezy-Cheeze sandwiches followed by Worcester sauce crisps. Her mum knows how to treat visitors and doesn't fuss if you accidentally spill apple juice on the tablecloth—no offence, Mrs Shepherd.

Thank you for listening. Now on to the subjects.

1. SCHOOL

Do you remember me saying Mrs Bent wouldn't let us go to see *Oliver!* because we weren't doing the

Victorians? Well, guess what? As soon as we've finished our Local Study project we can. Mrs Bent has booked tickets and is going to prepare us thoroughly for it. Mum says it's because of what Anthony did to me so Jem joked that our trip must be a guilt trip then. Why are grown-ups' jokes difficult to understand and not one bit funny?

Anyway, we watched the video of *Oliver!* yesterday and we're learning the songs. So now it's cold jelly and custard at home and at school. It's driving me mad. I asked Jem if Mayhem will  do *Grease* next time. Do you remember us doing the dance to 'Greased Lightning' at the Christmas disco?

You will be thrilled to know you can have your old tray again because Melanie is returning to Miss Cassidy's, her behaviour has improved so much. Mrs Bent says I've had a calming influence on her. I'm beginning to think Mum's right—Benty is creeping up to me. I even received a 'Super Work' stamp for my Trade in Bartock questionnaire but she says she can't put it on display because of Dad's answer to my question about rude magazines. He'd get on well with your gran would my dad, language-wise.

By the way, there's a boy in *Oliver!* called Sebastian. He's fifteen and once appeared in a Weetabix advert. Do you want me to send you a picture of him? I think he's your sort!

I know you won't mind me going on about it because it was an important day in my life.

Dad and Alexis's party was cool. It started off slowly because the caterers took the food to the Rugby Club by mistake and by the time they realized there were only two plates of tuna sandwiches and a curry dip left. We had to eat peanuts and pickled eggs all night.

Mel and me spent the first hour playing with Conan on the one-arm bandit until the landlord told us off for being under age but we had won 75p by then. It wasn't until Tarzan turned up that things really started happening.

You see, Toni, Mel's big sister who is Alexis's best friend, remember, never cancelled the Jane and Tarzan-a-grams she had bought Dad and Alexis as a wedding present. Jane couldn't come anyway because she'd twisted her ankle pretending to be Sally Gunnell at a Sport's Quiz on Thursday, but Tarzan came.

He burst through the door of the Function Room just as Dad was singing 'New York, New York' on the karaoke. Nobody took much notice at first because we were watching Dad and everyone thought it was him when Tarzan went 'ar-aha-ahar' . . . Then Tarzan spotted Alexis, who was swaying near to Dad, and ran up to her and swooped her up in his arms and ran off, leaving clumps of furry acrylic behind when his mini-skirt-thing got caught in Conan's pushchair handles. I recognized the acrylic because it was very similar to the stuff I chose for the Ugly Sisters' slippers.

We all stood round for ages, thinking they'd come running back through. Dad sang 'Knights in White Satin' followed by 'Raindrops Keep Falling on my Head' before it clicked that Alexis was missing. Even then he wasn't bothered and started chatting to Mum who'd come to pick me up early—she'd said ten and it was only quarter to.

Mel and me decided to sneak off so I wouldn't have to leave and guess what? We found Alexis and Tarzan under the pool table in the Games Room kissing like in films. I said, 'Hello, Alexis', and Mel said, 'Hello, Uncle LeeRoy.' You guessed it. Tarzan was really her Uncle LeeRoy who spends a lot of time on benches. We all sat under the pool table.

LeeRoy's real job is as a bouncer at 'Lazer Rave's' in town but that doesn't start until later so sometimes he's Tarzan and sometimes he's Rocky II but most of all he's Bond, James Bond, before he goes bouncing. He does Bond, James Bond at a lot of ladies' Divorce Parties and says they're the worst. He's always having to buy new dickie-bows. He was really funny, Mel's Uncle LeeRoy, once you learn to ignore the knife scars. Your gran would like him, but possibly not your dad and definitely not your mum.

Then Alexis asked us if we minded getting her a diet bitter lemon so we went but when we came back they'd gone again. We did find a note, written on the back of a 'Fungrams for all Okkasions' card that said 'Denny: If you won't swing me through the jungle someone else will. Lexy.' Except she'd missed the 'n' out of jungle.

When we showed Dad he just laughed and said to Mum, 'Well, Caffy, you were always saying I should do more for the environment.'

Then Mum laughed a bit sadly, not even telling him off for calling her 'Caffy' and leaned across and kissed Dad on the lips. I can't remember the last time she did that. I don't think I was even born. 'Poor Dennis,' she said.

Then we had to go, which was not fair because Mel was allowed to stay as long as she wanted and it was my dad's party after all.

Dennis walked us to the car, which took ages because he was drunk and kept falling over fresh air, and just as we were about to drive away he said, 'What about giving us another go, Caf? For Simone's sake? I really miss the little blossom,' and Mum stalled the engine and said, 'Stand back or you'll get run over,' which I thought was unfriendly. So I told him about the Super Work sticker but he was a man with a mission and went on, 'I'll change, Caffy, I'll wash up every night and only go to United's home matches . . . ' to which Mum replied, 'What about the drinking?' and Dad burped and said, 'What drinking?' so Mum just laughed and drove off.

Mum and me had a long talk when we got back about growing up and how she hoped I would be a strong person and do what I wanted to do in life and not be forced into things by other people. I said I would. I asked her if she wanted to marry Jem and set me a good example like your mum wrote. After calming down she shook her head and said no. She likes Jem very very much but she is happy going to college and being her own boss and not having to think about a third person. She likes it that Jem is away most of the time and gives her space. I admit I do, too. Jem is cool but when it is just the two of us, I can cuddle Mum whenever I want to without having an audience. I expect Mum will only ever go out with actors from now on.

Anyway, then Dad phoned to say that Alexis had come back and they were going for an Indian and probably would get married after all but not yet. I heard Mum say, 'Of course I won't say anything about what you said in the car park.'

It's funny but when Mum and Dad first split up I prayed every night that they would get back together but I'm glad now that they didn't. Alexis suits Dad and Jem suits Mum. When I grow up I'm not going to marry anyone until I make dead sure whoever gives me the look of love really means it and hasn't just got something in his eye.

Love from Simone

x xxxxxx x xx xx xx x xx xx x

PS   This goes under SCHOOL. We had to fill in a form for Bartock High and list three people we wanted to sit with in Year Seven. I put you first and Peter Bacon second and Joe P. third. I'm glad Melanie's only a Y5 or I'd have had problems. I also put *Not* Anthony Bent, in case he fails his exam for Alabaster Boys.

'Bally-Hi',
Harbour Ridge,
Sydney
Australia

May 26th

Dear Simone,
   That last letter was the longest anyone has ever
written to me. Gran read it, too, when I was in the
bath and couldn't stop her. I could hear her laughing
all the way down the hall. She said to tell you if
LeeRoy ever wanted a place to stay he's welcome to
stay here with her in 'Bally Hi' but DON'T YOU
DARE. Knowing her, she'd marry him then I'd be
related to the McCleods. Can you imagine!
   I still promise to act normal when I return and we
are a three with Melanie. I won't call her anything or
make you choose between us. That would be so unfair
on poor Melanie and you did put me down as your
number one friend for Bartock High, so that tells me
everything I need to know.
   I haven't much news. I've hardly seen Mummy and
Daddy this week because they went to Wogga Wogga
with the Lings for a seminar on 'Chemicals in
Cleaning—do they rot the brain?' I wish they would
talk to me properly like your parents and Jem do. It's
the only thing you've got that I haven't, although I
have to admit Gran does treat me like an adult. She
has bought me a trainer bra. It's a proper bra, not a
crop top. I think they are only available in Australia.
   I would like a photograph of Sebastian. There are
no nice boys round here at all. Post it quick, though, or

it might not arrive in time. Here's Anthony's letter back. What a wally!

We are all going to Bondi Beach this weekend to watch Gran in a surfing competition. It will be our last event before packing up to come home. Save me a place in the theatre for *Oliver!* I'm sure Jem will make a good effort.

Love from Chloe Madelaine Shepherd.

A very good friend indeed

The News Shack,
45 High Street,
Bartock.

June 3rd

Dear Chloe,

Merci beaucoup for the letter and then the postcard of Bondi Beach. You must be proud of your gran winning the surfing competition. My nana won't even watch *Baywatch* in case she gets her slippers wet.

This is probably the last letter I'll write to you before you come back to Bartock. Notice anything strange about the address? That's right, I'm living with my dad for two weeks. My mum is helping Jem in *Oliver!* because it's a disaster and he needs someone normal with him. I think she's really gone to spy on Nancy, (Queen Stretchy-Lycra) in case she tries any funny stuff. The deal is Cathryn does two weeks in *Oliver!* and Jem does two weeks cleaning her offices, all the washing and all the cooking when *Oliver!*'s finished. He thinks he's got the easy part. He has no idea. I've been to those offices Mum cleans. I've seen his future.

Mum phones every night before the evening performance. She says the play's not as bad as Jem makes out but it lacks atmosphere. I told her she'd never sat through one of our assemblies.

I'm missing home but it's fun living above the News Shack. We have take-away food nearly every night because Alexis is allergic to ovens. She's allergic to irons, too, so Dad had to press my sweatshirt for school but he made the iron too hot and melted the motto.

Alexis and Dad just watch telly at night and don't talk much. Dad says it's good practice for when they get married. The best bit is I can go to bed really late and watch *The Bill* but I'm not allowed to breathe a word during *Coronation Street*.

It's hard getting to sleep at night because I worry about burglars. The News Shack is always having break-ins because Dad's alarm fell off the front wall and everyone can see it was only a box cover and not real in the first place. In fact, it was another of his false alarms—ha-ha! For protection I take Cakebread and Spotty to bed with me and they help to make me feel safe. Cakebread has settled back in England, you'll be pleased to know.

Melanie slept over last night. We had a brilliant time down in the shop after it had closed. We played shop assistant and rude customer then customer and rude shop assistant and ate loads of penny mixtures until we felt sick. It would have been miles better if you had been here because then we could have had two rude customers at once. I'm glad you are going to be OK with her.

Jem has sent me this picture of Sebastian. Before you ask, I don't know what that thing is on the side of his face either. It could be sideburns. It could be

Weetabix. Do you think he's better looking than that student we had, Mr Cohen?

I've also written out all the words to the *Oliver!* songs for you so you can join in when we go and see it. We sound really good when we're practising in the hall, especially now we've got the new keyboards from the supermarket vouchers. Miss Cassidy says we could make our own CD and sell it on Parents' Evenings. I'm going to phone Jem and see if he'll let us sing on stage with him. That way, the school will have money and *Oliver!* will have atmosphere.

I have also had a brilliant idea for the gruel. Poor Oliver has to eat cold porridge twice a day which is child abuse if you ask me so I've made up a recipe using two parts banana Angel Whip and one part Ready Brek. I think it'll be another winner, like the flying toes.

I'll save you a place in the chorus but you will have to practise the words. Jem is very fussy about knowing the right words and so is Miss Cassidy.

See you later, alligator . . .

Simone

June 10th

Hi Simone,

As you can see I'm still here. We should have set off three days ago but Daddy had an accident so we had to postpone the flight and change the tickets. He was trying to surf better than Grandma and crashed into a rock. He broke his ankle and scraped his shins. Some of the skin from his leg was stuck to the rock. Grandma said it served him right for being so childish.

I'm not too bothered about missing *Oliver!* because I've seen it done properly in London but I am worried someone else might steal my tray now that Melanie's been sent back to Miss Cassidy's. Mrs Bent never did reply to Mummy's letter, you know.

Mummy says you must sleep over at our house when we return so that we can rekindle our friendship. She suggests you don't tell Melanie though. I don't mind letting her hang out with us at school but after school is different. No offence but two's company, three's a crowd and you and I always get on best when we're alone together, don't we? I know you'll understand. Mummy has some very valuable pieces of jewellery in the house.

Thank you for the picture of Sebastian. I think he's fairly handsome but Mr Cohen was better.

From Chlo (notice no 'e' now, please) your true best friend x xxxxxx x xx xx xx x xx x *sorry forgot*

1 Council House Lane,
Little Woodhill,
Nr. Bartock.

June 13th

Dear Chloé,

You have just missed the best week of school ever!
Jem loved my idea about us singing in the chorus and
Mrs Bent agreed almost straightaway so *Oliver!* was
brilliant, thanks to us. We even had a write-up and
photograph in the *Bartock Post*. I was interviewed on
my own. A reporter called Kelly asked me how I
came up with the idea. She made loads of notes and
even wrote down my recipe for the gruel jelly. I had
my photograph taken with Sebastian (he was the
Artful Dodger) and the rest of the cast.

Dad bought a proper copy from the paper and he's
having it enlarged for the shop window. He says it's
to cover a crack in the glass but I know he's proud
of me really. He's been a changed man since the
Father's Day card incident; not missed custardy
time once.

In the play we all had to wear raggy clothes and
smother our faces in grime to look like urchins
(except Peter Bacon thought we meant sea urchins
and wore his sister's pink leotard—no comment).
We performed in front of tons of schools every
afternoon and twice on the Saturday, literally.

We had a party with pop and Pringles afterwards
and Jem danced with Mrs Bent! He twirled her

round so high we could see her knickers! They were lemon.

Jem said ticket sales were higher in Bartock than anywhere else and wanted the school to go to Lyme Regis with them but Mrs Bent said we had to get back to Handling Data. Jem asked if they had a theatre there but Mrs Bent had returned to normal and didn't find it funny.

Mum and Jem have got the look of love as strong as ever. Sally Smith didn't even bother to stay to the party. I guess she knew there was no point, especially as Mum enjoyed her two weeks with Mayhem Theatre Company so much she is thinking about helping out with dance routines and fitness warm-ups next time.

I wish you had been with us on stage instead of waiting for your dad's ankle to heal but tell him he'll be glad to know his shops have been closing early as a mark of respect.

This next bit is hard for me to write which is why I wrote so much about the play, I suppose. I was avoiding the issue. Mum says Dad does that a lot. I guess I take after him. Anyway, here goes.

Remember how I promised Mum after Dad's party I wouldn't let other people push me around? Well, I'm sorry to say that means you, Chlo. I'm finding it harder and harder to stay friends with you. Mainly it is because you are nasty about Melanie. Every time I open one of your letters I wonder what you are going to say next and I know it won't be good. When I used to open Jem's letters I had a warm feeling in my stomach but when I open yours, my stomach gets all knotted, like it used to when Mum argued with Dad.

Listen, Mel wouldn't dream of stealing your mum's jewels like you implied in your last letter. Maybe she does wear clothes that are too small for her and has relatives who are in jail and loses her temper sometimes but she has a lot of good things about her. If you don't want to be friends with Melanie, that's up to you but I have the right to choose who I play with, no offence.

She read a couple of your letters—she is a nosy parker and no mistake—but she burst into tears before I could have a go at her. You know how tough she is, Chlo—McCleods never cry. I was smitten with shock, I can tell you. So now I've got her worrying I won't be friends with her when you come back and you worrying I won't be just friends with you when you do. I feel like my brain is going to splatter further than the Ugly Sister's toes did in *Cinderella*.

I've been thinking about this a lot and I am really, really fed up with being piggy-in-the-middle. First I was piggy with Mum and Dad, then with Dad and Alexis and a bit with Mum and Jem and now with you and Melanie. You have never been piggy because your parents did not separate when you were seven nearly eight like mine did. It's no fun and I'm not going to do it with my friends as well as my relatives. Kids ought to know better.

So I have prepared some tips for you and Mel for when you return. This idea worked for Jem with Mum, so maybe it will work for us. If you sign the tips, it means you agree to them, if you don't it means you don't want to be friends with me any more. I hope you sign—Melanie did in a flash, which is why her signature's such a mess. I don't like falling out, it makes me feel shaky and sad but I will understand if you want to hang out with Kayleigh B. or someone instead. I know sharing is difficult for dry cleaners' children.

As Mel thought up number three, you can put one of your own in for number six.

Here goes.

TIPS FOR HANGING OUT IN THREES

1.   Everyone takes turns to decide what to play.

2.   If one of us gets invited to tea and the other doesn't, it's OK as long as no one goes on and on about it.

3.   Nobody makes comments about jails or benches.

4.   Only give presents if you are sure you don't want them back. It saves unhappiness.

5.   Two people will not try to make the other one feel left out or unwanted or thwarted.

6.

We agree to these terms and conditions

signed: Simone Anna Wibberley

signed: Melanie McCleod

signed:

Looking forward to hearing your reply.

Sketchley Ho.,
New Estate Rd.,
Little Woodhill
Bartock.

June 25th

TO: Simone

I am looking forward to having tea at your house tomorrow even if Jem is doing the cooking. I know actors can cook because I've seen *Under Seige* with Steven Segal five times. It's a 15.

Just to let you know my gran bought us all (me, you, and Melanie McC.) an authentic wooden pencil box, carved by real aborigines, complete with didgeridoo-shaped biros which I'll bring with me. She also sent you a book on Time. I assured her you would appreciate it.

Anyway, I have signed your document, though Daddy said it would not stand up in a court of law. Please note my number 6 is more for Melanie than you.

FROM: Chlo your friend from way back.

TIPS FOR HANGING OUT IN THREES

1. Everyone takes turns to decide what to play.

2. If one of us gets invited to tea and the other doesn't, it's OK as long as no one goes on and on about it.

3. Nobody makes comments about jails or benches.

4. Only give presents if you are sure you don't want them back. It saves unhappiness.

5. Two people will not try to make the other one feel left out or unwanted or thwarted.

6. Nobody takes anything that doesn't belong to them.

We agree to these terms and conditions

signed: _Simone Anna Wibberley_

signed: _Melanie McCleod_

signed: _C. M. Shepherd_

Looking forward to hearing your reply.

1 Council House Lane,
Little Woodhill,
Nr. Bartock
England

July 1st

Dear Chloe's Gran,

Sorry I don't know your name but Chloe isn't speaking to me and wouldn't tell me it but I wanted to write to thank you very much for the didgeridoo pencil box and the book called *All You Need To Know About Time and Space*. I am saving the book for when I go on holiday to Scotland with Mum and Jem in summer. We are going camping near a loch. A loch is a lake not a lock like on your door, in case you didn't know. It is the first holiday I have had since my parents split up when I was seven nearly eight so you can imagine how excited I am.

The didgeridoo pencil case is very well designed and crafted. Trust me, I know about these things. I will use it every day when I get to Bartock High. Thank you.

I hope you don't mind me writing even though your granddaughter is not speaking to me. What happened was, she came to tea which should have been fun because Jem had made his special pasta bake and Melanie wasn't even there because she was baby-sitting for Conan while Toni went to the shops. Chloe was fine at first, but then she said she wanted Cakebread back because after all you had sent me so many things. I refused and reminded her she had signed the agreement which included number four.

She got into a real mardy and wouldn't touch the pasta bake or laugh at her tray which I had sneaked out of class at great danger to myself and decorated with a silk ribbon. Well, I'm sorry, Gran Shepherd, but I couldn't be bothered wasting time any more so I telephoned your son at his shop and asked him to pick Chloe up a.s.a.p. which he did. He was even more mardy than Chloe because he'd been in the middle of starching the mayor's new curtains.

She did telephone afterwards and said sorry but I have a feeling it was one of those sorrys your parents force you to say when you don't really mean it, deep down. At school she has been OK but not over-friendly. We're supposed to be designing the parents' programme for the Leavers' Service together but if you want to know the truth, I've done it all on my own. I don't really mind, though; I can work independently or part of a group—it said so on my report. Here's a sneak preview of my programme. I plan to have an empty page at the back so everyone can write their farewell messages like this: I have chosen the font Rockwell Bold because Norman Rockwell is Miss Cassidy's favourite artist.

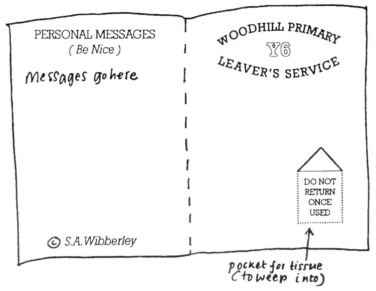

It's a shame you can't come to the Leavers' Service. Your son, Mr Shepherd, has business commitments so only your daughter-in-law, Mrs Shepherd, will be there and she could have done with the company. My whole gang are coming to see me: Mum, Jem, Dad, Alexis, and even Melanie, as an honorary Y6. I'm reading out a poem called 'Goodbye Woodhill Primary', It goes like this:

Goodbye, Woodhill Primary School,
My time with you's been really cool.
I'll miss the teachers
All warm and friendly
But I don't think I'll miss assembly.

The toffee trip made me ill
But doing *Oliver!* was a thrill.
Weren't Victorians really cruel
For making kids eat stuff called gruel?

My favourite teacher was Miss Cassidy
Because she was so very nice to me.
When my parents got divorced
She helped me through the very worst.

Mrs Bent started off real mardy
But got better at the *Oliver!* party.
She's still stingy with her stickers
Because she wears those lemon knickers.

To Melanie I just want to say
I'm so glad you got Chloe's tray.
I used to think you were a geek
But now I know you are unique.

I started here when I was seven
And when I leave I'll be eleven.
Now my time here is at an end
I go with joy and my new friends.
Bye, then, Woodhill Primary School,
Like I said, you're really cool.

by Simone Wibberley aged nearly 11

Mrs Bent hasn't had time to check the poem yet but I
think she'll like the way I rhymed everything.

Good luck with any more surfing competitions.
LeeRoy McCleod is still available for dates, if you're
interested.

With very best wishes,

Simone Anna Wibberley

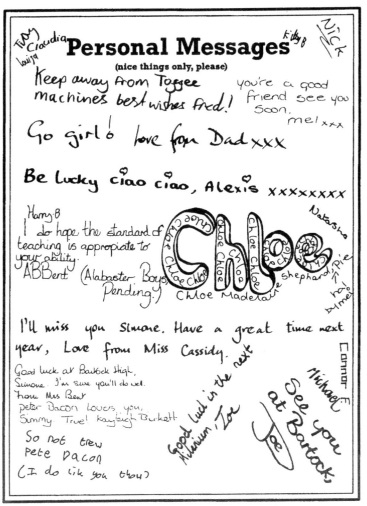

Personal Messages

(nice things only, please)

Tippy Claudia Luija Kirby B NICK

Keep away from Toggee machines best wishes Fred!

you're a good friend see you soon.
mel xxx

Go girl! love from Dad xxx

Be lucky ciao ciao, Alexis xxxxxxxx

Harry B
I do hope the standard of teaching is appropriate to your ability.
ABBent (Alabaster Boys Pending.)

Chloe Chloe Chloe Chloe Chloe Chloe Chloe Chloe Chloe Chloe Chloe Madelaine

Natasha
Shephard Pie
Roo Dimer

I'll miss you Simone. Have a great time next year, Love from Miss Cassidy.

Good luck at Bawlock High, Simone. I'm sure you'll do well.
from Mrs Bent
peter Bacon loves you, Simmy. True! Kayleigh Birkett

So not true
PETE BACON
(I do lik you thou)

Good luck in the next Millenium, Zoe

Connor F

Michael
See you at Bawlocks
Joe

---

designed by Simone A. Wibberley

I am so proud of you Simone
Love and lots of hugs
Mum xx —x

I am literally smitten by your talent, Miss Wibberley. Have a zillion Super work stickers.
Jem x

Also by Helena Pielichaty

Vicious Circle

ISBN 0 19 271775 8

Ten-year-old Louisa May and her mother Georgette are two of the 'have-nots', shuttling between ever-seedier bed and breakfast accommodation. To help cope they play elaborate fantasy games, pretending to be the characters in romantic fiction.

When they arrive at the Cliff Top Villas Hotel and Georgette falls ill, it looks as if the fantasy will have to end. But Louisa May determines to find out the truth behind Georgette's 'let's pretend' existence. Maybe there will be a chance for them to break out of the vicious circle and become 'haves' at last . . .

'the story is told with a strong sense of humour and is highly readable.'

Newark Advertiser

Getting Rid of Karenna

ISBN 0 19 271819 3

Even now Suzanne could remember the fear, the humiliation, the pain, caused by the constant bullying; the two year reign of terror in which she had been driven to the brink of a breakdown. It is three years since Karenna left the school and Suzanne is beginning to put it all behind her, but suddenly Karenna has come back into her life. Is it all going to begin again? Will she never be free of the nightmare? In order to get on with her own life, Suzanne has to find some way to rid herself of the past . . . of Karenna.